DIVE INTO READING!

Block Party

Henry   Lily   Mei   Pablo   Padma

by Gwendolyn Hooks

illustrated by Sh

D1041878

Lee & Low Books Inc. New York

Thank you, Kim Ventrella, for that perfect line—G.H.

To Renee, the best neighbor and baker, who makes
every party delicious!—S.N-B.

Copyright © 2017 by Lee & Low Books Inc.
All rights reserved. No part of this book may be reproduced, transmitted, or stored in
an information retrieval system in any form or by any means, electronic, mechanical,
photocopying, recording, or otherwise, without written permission from the publisher.
LEE & LOW BOOKS Inc., 95 Madison Avenue, New York, NY 10016
leeandlow.com
Book design by Kimi Weart
Book production by The Kids at Our House
The illustrations are rendered in watercolor and enhanced digitally
Manufactured in China by Imago, January 2018
Printed on paper from responsible sources
(hc) 10 9 8 7 6 5 4 3 2 1
(pb) 10 9 8 7 6 5 4 3 2
First Edition

Library of Congress Cataloging-in-Publication Data
Names: Hooks, Gwendolyn, author. | Ng-Benitez, Shirley, illustrator.
Title: Block party / by Gwendolyn Hooks; illustrated by Shirley Ng-Benitez.
Description: First edition. | New York: Lee & Low Books, [2017]
Series: Dive into reading; 3 | Summary: "The neighborhood is having a block
party and everyone is expected to bring food to share. Padma's mother decides
to bring a pot of homemade soup, and Padma worries that her friends will not
like it"—Provided by publisher.
Identifiers: LCCN 2016028088 | ISBN 9781620143414 (hardcover: alk. paper)
ISBN 9781620143421 (pbk.: alk. paper)
Subjects: | CYAC: Parties—Fiction. | Neighborhoods—Fiction. |
Play—Fiction. | Food—Fiction.
Classification: LCC PZ7.H76635 Bl 2017 | DDC [E]—dc23
LC record available at https://lccn.loc.gov/2016028088

Contents

The Note

Padma saw a note on the door.

"A block party!" said Padma.
She ran inside to tell her mom.

"What is a block party?"
asked Padma.

"It's a party with the neighbors,"
said her mom.
"People will bring food to share."

"Let's bring pizza," said Padma.
"Let's bring our lentil soup,"
said her mom.
"I learned to make it in India."

"Oh no, Mom," said Padma.
"No one will like our lentil soup."

Hiding Place

Padma looked out the window.
She didn't see any soup.

"No one brings soup
to a block party," said Padma.

"Please take the pot of soup outside," said Padma's mom. "Dad and I will be there soon."

Padma looked for a place to hide the pot of soup.

Padma saw her friends
Henry, Mei, Lily, and Pablo.

"Let's go on the slide,"
said Lily.

They jumped in the castle.
Padma jumped high.

They played hide-and-seek.
Padma hid under a table.
Henry found her.

Lunchtime

"I'm hungry," said Henry.
"Let's eat!"

They looked at all the different foods.
Padma hoped they wouldn't find
the lentil soup.

They ate rice and beans.
They ate corn on the cob.
They ate egg rolls.
They ate fish and chips.

Everyone ate the different foods.

"Look!" said Lily.
"Here is a pot of soup."

Padma didn't look at the soup.
"But there are no bowls,"
said Lily.

"Here are the bowls and spoons,"
said Padma's mom.

"I'm ready for soup," said Mei. Padma was sure Mei wouldn't like the lentil soup.

"Here's a bowl of soup for you,"
said Henry.
Padma took the bowl.

No one talked.
Padma was sure her friends
didn't like the lentil soup.

"Who made the soup?" asked Lily.
"My mom and I made it,"
said Padma.
"She learned to make the soup
in India."

"It's so good!" said Lily.
"I wish there was more,"
said Henry.

Padma smiled a big smile.
"Come to my house tomorrow,"
she said.
"My mom will help us
make more lentil soup."

It was the best lentil soup ever!

Lentil Curry Soup

You can make your own delicious lentil soup.
Be sure to have an adult help you.

Serves 4

Ingredients

2 cups broth   3 TBS curry spice mix
1/2 cup red lentils   1-1/2 cups coconut milk

1. Place broth in a 2-quart pot and heat on medium high heat until boiling.
2. Sort and rinse well the lentils, then add lentils and curry spice mix to broth. Stir.
3. Cover pot with lid. Simmer on medium low heat for about 15 minutes. Check occasionally and stir gently to keep lentils from sticking to bottom of pot.
4. Add coconut milk. Stir, cover pot with lid, and cook until lentils are tender.

Options:
• Vegetable or chicken broth may be used.
• Add any diced vegetables or chopped cooked chicken when lentils are added to broth.
• Garnish with dollop of plain yogurt and small pieces of fresh parsley.

recipe by Donna Jackson Campbell Brice, Home Economist